Christmas Vows
$5 Extra

Christmas Vows
$5⁰⁰ EXTRA

best-selling author

LORI COPELAND

Tyndale House Publishers, Inc., Wheaton, Illinois

Library of Congress Cataloging-in-Publication Data

Copeland, Lori.
   Christmas vows: $5.00 extra / Lori Copeland
      p. cm.—(HeartQuest)
   ISBN 0-8423-5326-7 (pbk.)
   1. Single-parent families—Fiction. 2. Ex-convicts—Fiction. I. Title.
II. Series.
PS3553.O6336 C49 2001
813'.54—dc21   2001001934

T*he old transmission went squirrelly twenty miles outside of Memphis.*

Snow pelted the windshield, and the Mercury's worn wiper blades could hardly keep up with the icy slush.

Ben O'Keefe swerved the car to the shoulder of I-55 North, startling the sleeping baby in the backseat from a deep sleep. Wails erupted.

Two wide-eyed faces popped up over the front seat, the two older children awake now, too.

"What's wrong, Daddy?" five-year-old Chris asked.

"Are we at Nana's yet?" Six-year-old Jody fisted sleep from her oval-shaped eyes.

Coasting to a stop on the shoulder, Ben set the emergency brake, turning to quiet little Peg with his right hand. "It's okay, sweetheart."

"Do we got anofer flat?" The boy hung over the passenger seat, peering at his dad.

"I'm not sure, Chris—I think it may be the transmission this time." Bands had been slipping for the last thirty miles; the pump wasn't going to last much longer.

Cars rumbled past, rattling the old car's chassis. Headlights pierced the snow as they flashed by the stranded vehicle.

Looking at his children, Ben calmed their fears. "Everything is fine. Daddy needs to get out of the car and take a look at the problem. Jody, give the baby her bottle. Chris, you help your sister. Don't anyone get out of this car. Do you understand?"

Nodding in somber unison, the two older children murmured, "Okay, Daddy."

Ben climbed out, pulling the collar of his worn Levi's jacket tighter against the wintry assault. The weather had steadily worsened the last hundred miles, and his nerves were stretched raw. Still sporting his prison pallor, he huddled against a cutting wind and stepped to the back of the vehicle. No emergency flare, no cell phone to call for help. Flagging down a passing motorist was laughable—any self-protecting citizen would be afraid to stop for fear he was a criminal—

A bitter laugh escaped him. What kind of a dad could he be to these innocent children?

Ben knew what kind of a dad he was—a desperate one. A man who'd just finished an eighteen-month stint in Tipton Correctional Center, released early to assume custody of his three children after their mom's death two months earlier. A man trying his level best to raise three small kids alone and trust fully in God's grace, but doing a mighty poor job of it so far.

Christmas lights winked from a golden arch a couple of miles up the highway. Well-fed children dressed in Old Navy or Gap pajamas would be sitting in warm

homes, ears tuned to the ten o'clock news, noses pressed to windowpanes, praying the snowfall would be heavy enough to put anticipated new sleds to good use.

Ben O'Keefe's kids didn't have a warm home, and they were hungry. No Gap pajamas—just frayed sleepers faded from too many washings. This snow was one more problem to handle.

Dropping to his knees, Ben bent just behind the left front wheel to study the transmission. Oil dripped from the pan. Sticking his finger in the hole to check the flow, he realized he wasn't going to make Poplar Bluff tonight; he'd be lucky to make it to the nearest garage.

Great, he thought. He had exactly two hundred and eighty-nine dollars and some change in his pocket, not to mention two little kids who'd eaten nothing but peanut-butter-and-jelly sandwiches for the last six hundred miles. The kids needed a hot meal, a bath, and a warm bed, but Nana's house in Poplar Bluff, Missouri, was still three hours away.

Pushing to his feet, he dodged a missile flung from the rear window. "Chris!" he yelled. "Stop wasting bread!"

"It's crust!"

Ben opened the back door and cranked up the window. "You're letting the heat out, son. Keep the window shut." Doing a double take, Ben frowned. "Where'd that dog come from?"

Chris shrugged, draping his arm affectionately around the mangiest-looking mutt Ben had ever laid eyes on. The animal's fur was soaked, and it stunk. "He just climbed in the car with me, Daddy. Right now. Can I keep him?"

"No."

A semi flashed by, throwing muck all over Ben and the windshield. Wiping his eyes with the back of his hand, he took a deep breath.

The car's interior stunk to high heaven. The dog had rolled in something foul. The baby squalled, wanting free of her dirty diaper. Holding his breath, Ben fumbled on the back floorboard for the Pampers. The mutt he'd take care of later. Right now he had his hands full adjusting to full-time parenting.

Three weeks ago he'd been handed his release papers and a bus ticket home. Home being Saint Louis, Missouri—or it was until his wife, Sheila, died. Sheila's sister, Lil, had taken the kids, so after his release, Ben

headed for Mobile, Alabama, to get them. He and the kids spent a couple of weeks in Mobile getting re-acquainted. Mom wanted them home for Christmas, so Ben was on the last leg of the trip when the transmission started giving him trouble.

I'm doing the best I can, Sheila. If you can give me any help from up there, I'd sure appreciate it.

The baby cooed, flashing Ben a gummy grin as he pulled her from the car seat and laid her below the steering wheel to change her diaper. He was getting good at this—thirty seconds flat, and dirty diaper was gone, Peg's bottom wiped and smeared with Diaper Doo, clean diaper in place.

"Yeah, you think it's all pretty funny, don't you," he teased, trying to protect her from the wind blowing in the open door.

"This dog is really neat, huh, Dad? And I don't think he has a home—he looks kind of like he's lost," said Chris.

He looks more kind of like he's been hit by a fast-moving freight and has lived to tell about it. Ben put Peg back in her car seat and glanced to see if the animal was wearing identification tags. He wasn't.

"Can I keep him, huh?" Chris peered at Ben hopefully. "It wouldn't be nice of us to leave him here on the highway with it snowing and all. He'll get sick."

"He probably lives nearby, son."

Chris shook his head. "I don't think so." He peered deep into the dog's eyes. "Do you live nearby?" He glanced back at Ben. "He don't. He wants to live with us."

Preoccupied, Ben let his thoughts drift. Christmas was two days off. What kind of Christmas could he give the kids this year? Sheila's doctor bills had wiped them out. She'd worked as a waitress the last couple of years, barely managing to hold things together. They'd never scraped enough money together to buy a house, so it had been easy to vacate the rented trailer. He'd given the old furniture to Goodwill and packed the kids' clothes and toys in brown paper sacks. Mom wasn't in much better shape; she lived on social security and her heart was giving her trouble again, but she'd said that he was welcome to stay with her until he found work.

Ben O'Keefe was twenty-eight, had a basic high school education and a prison record. Job prospects weren't exactly limitless, but he was strong, dependable, and good with his hands. He could work Manpower temp jobs if needed until he found something. He wasn't that crazy kid anymore who'd gotten involved in a convenience-store holdup; he'd learned his lesson. The past eighteen months had reeducated his values. Incarceration had taught him two things: He was not smarter than anyone else, and Jesus Christ died on the cross for his sins. The latter blew his mind when he thought about it, and he'd decided early on that since he could never repay the debt, he intended to spend his life trying to live up to God's expectations.

This Christmas wouldn't be the best his kids ever had, but they would have each other. Raising three kids alone wasn't going to be easy, but he could do it, with God's help.

"The dog stays here, Chris." Ben pulled the mutt out of the car over the children's yelps of protests. Cars whizzed by, throwing brackish slush on the Mercury.

Ben climbed back behind the wheel and started the engine, easing back into traffic. The old engine bucked and jerked until he got it wound out and running.

Chris and Jody pressed their noses against the back window, watching the dog gradually fade from sight.

If Ben remembered correctly there was a garage before the U.S. 412 exit—if the old car could make it that far. He glanced in the rearview mirror. Chris was still mourning the dog, his head hung low.

Don't let sympathy get to you, Ben. You've got enough problems without adding a stray mutt to the mix.

Jody leaned over and halfheartedly balanced a bottle in the baby's mouth. Milk dripped from Peg's chin and soaked the front of her shirt. The little girl stared at Ben with soulful eyes.

Ben reached back and steadied the bottle. "Keep it in Sissy's mouth, Jody."

"He wouldn't eat much, Daddy," Chris pleaded. "He could have some of my food." They were back to the dog.

The old heater made a strange noise. *Please, God, don't let the bearing go out until I can get the kids somewhere.*

Jody sighed, turning to look at her brother, who was still staring out the back window with a long face, tears rolling silently down his cheeks. "Daddy?"

Slamming on the brakes, Ben made a U-turn and gunned the old car back down the highway in a boil of

smoke and a slipping clutch. Screeching to a halt beside the dog, he opened the passenger door. The half-frozen mutt lunged into the Mercury and settled into the backseat between Peg and Chris. Tongue lolling to one side, he cocked his head and stared straight ahead, instantly part of the O'Keefe family.

The kids' excited chatter overrode Ben's strong but silent objection as he set off again. Three kids and a mangy dog. He must be out of his mind.

The dog reared on the backseat, putting his front paws near Ben's ear. Ben quickly cracked a window for air.

"Daddy?"

"Yes, Jody?"

"I'm hungry."

"There's peanut butter and bread in the sack."

Chris heaved a sigh. "We've eated that all day." The child's eyes fastened on the large golden arches straight ahead. "French fries," he murmured with a trace of longing.

"French fries," Jody echoed with the same tangible yearning. She leaned closer. "Can we have some French fries, Daddy?"

Ben thought about the money in his pocket: two hundred eighty-nine dollars and some change—every cent Sheila had in the house when she died. Hamburgers and French fries were out of the question if he were to make the money last until he got a job. The gas needle hovered on a quarter of a tank. If he found a garage, it wouldn't be open tonight, so that meant unless they slept in the car he'd have to find a Super 8 Motel.

Thirty bucks for a bed and heat. He shook his head to clear the cobwebs. He'd have to find the garage and pray that the owner would take mercy on his situation.

Yeah, mercy for an ex-con. Unlikely, Ben. Highly unlikely.

Snow fell in sheets as Ben leaned closer to the wheel, concentrating on the road. The Mercury bucked down the highway, trailing black smoke. The transmission would go any minute.

Jody pressed her mouth against Ben's ear and whispered, "French fries."

"We can't spare the money, sweetheart." To refuse her broke his heart, but he'd let them have the dog, whose snores now filled the backseat.

How much did French fries cost—a buck or less?

11

But they'd need every cent for gas. If the transmission went out, he'd have to sell the car for whatever he could get for a '73 Mercury with two hundred thousand plus on the odometer and no transmission.

Glowing McDonald's lights loomed ahead. Persistent now, Jody hovered over the front seat and eyed the golden arch, getting closer. "I'm sooooooo hungry, Daddy."

Pressed next to the wheel, Ben fished in his pocket for change, keeping an eye on worsening road conditions. If he had ninety cents in change he'd pull up at the drive-through window. The dash light enabled him to count nickels, dimes, and pennies. A quarter, three dimes, four nickels . . . one, two . . . five . . . nine . . . ten pennies.

Eighty-five cents.

Eighty-five stinkin' cents. He glanced over his shoulder to meet two expectant gazes.

"French fries, Daddy."

"No," he said, steeling his jaw. "I'm a nickel short." He mashed down harder on the gas, and the old car shot past the McDonald's entrance. Two days before Christmas, and he was a nickel short—the story of his life.

12

The kids quieted, their heads whipping to watch the large clown gradually fade out of sight.

Dropping into the backseat, they sat pensively, their solemn faces reflected in the passing car lights.

Ben's conscience throbbed. French fries. He couldn't buy his kids a bag of French fries. The chaplain's words rang in his head: *"It's not going to be easy out there, Ben, but God will be with you. That is his promise. Be faithful to him and he will be faithful to you."*

I'm doing the best I can—and I'm willing to give it all I've got, but I need your help, Lord. Bad, Ben prayed silently.

He ignored the sudden sound of backseat activities as one of the children rummaged around in sacks and sifted through trash on the floorboard. The dog popped up on the back of his seat again.

Suddenly, Jody's head emerged, and a tooth-gapped grin dominated her babyish features. "Look, Daddy! A nickel!"

Glancing over his shoulder, Ben spotted the shiny coin she was holding midair. "Where did you get that?"

"In the seat! I pushed my hand in the cracks like

Mommy used to do and I found it!" Eyes brightened. "Now can we have French fries?"

Swerving to the right shoulder, Ben caught a break in traffic and made a wide U-turn. The worn transmission bands slipped as the tires grabbed for traction. Squealing with glee, the children clapped their hands, and a holiday-like atmosphere prevailed as Ben, the kids, and the dog drove the short distance back to McDonald's.

Engine racing, he chugged up to the drive-through window in third gear and drew a fair number of curious stares. Ben let the motor idle as he waited at the speaker box.

"Welcome to McDonald's. Would you like to try our Big Mac Biggie combo tonight?"

"No, one small fries, please."

Crackle . . . crackle . . . "Try a hot apple pie with that, sir?" . . . *crackle.*

"No, just the fries," Ben said.

"Anything to drink?"

"No, just the fries."

Jody hung over the backseat, hovering near Ben's right ear. "Can't she hear, Daddy?"

Crackle . . . crackle . . . "Large coke and one small fries . . ."

"No, one small fries and nothing to drink."

Crackle . . . crackle . . . "Dr. Pepper . . . can I super-size that for you?"

"No." Ben took a deep breath. "One small fries. No drink."

Crackle . . . crackle . . . "Eight . . ." *Crackle.* "Cents . . . pull around to the drive-through window . . ."

Smoke boiled from underneath the old Mercury and obscured the young attendant's face as Ben handed her a fistful of change.

Coughing, she counted the pennies and nickels, her eyes peering through the blue haze at the smoking spectacle.

Ben smiled. "Keep the change."

She disappeared and came back a moment later, stuffing a handful of napkins in the paper sack. When she handed the order out the window, she remained a safe distance back.

"Thanks." Ben opened the sack; when he saw two large orders of fries, he groaned. The tantalizing smell of the crispy hot potato sticks filled the car's interior. Peg

stirred, opening her eyes, her hand palm out in a gimme gesture.

Ben handed the sack back through the window. "There's two large fries in here; I ordered a small one."

Smiling, the girl winked. "My mistake, sir. Enjoy the fries. Merry Christmas!"

She slammed the window shut, coughing.

Two large orders of fries. Ben bit back tears as he pulled away. They could each eat their fill. The kids dug in. Ben blew on a fry to cool it down, then handed it to an eager Peg. Dog got into the act, sniffing the sack.

"Thank you, God," he acknowledged as the old Mercury bucked back onto the highway and he bit into a hot, crispy fry, pitching one to the dog.

I never appreciated teenage help more.

I f there ever had been a garage on exit 60, it wasn't
there now.

No garage, Lord. Are you looking? I sure need your help.

It was close to midnight, the kids were asleep, and a
long stretch of deserted highway lay ahead. Ben couldn't
risk the transmission holding together long enough to
make Poplar Bluff tonight.

He turned the Mercury off the highway and

motored up a long snow-covered lane. He caught a brief glance at a sign but couldn't read the message. Something about parlor . . . marrying.

The old car bumped along the rutted road, jostling its occupants. The baby's head bobbed at a lopsided angle in the backseat; the other kids curled in a tight knot against each door, kicking Peg's car seat when they moved. Dog snored peacefully on the floor.

The four bald tires barely made it up the snow-packed lane. The car died a coughing death thirty feet from a towering farmhouse. The monstrosity looked like Herman and Lily Munster's house. Ben sat in the stillness, staring at a sign flapping wildly above the gabled porch:

THE MARRYING PARLOR
HENRIETTA HUMBLESMITH, PROPRIETOR
(CHRISTMAS VOWS: $5.00 EXTRA)

Ben didn't need vows, but he sure needed a warm bed and a decent breakfast for his kids.

Please God, let someone be home.

Headlights illuminated the parlor's front door, which by now had been flung open to reveal a tall, raw-boned woman with protruding teeth—the old Ben

would have called them buckteeth—and hair rolled in curlers that looked to be small orange-juice cans. She was wearing a ratty-looking, red chenille bathrobe and pointing a .410 shotgun straight at him. Her squirrel-like eyes stared down the sight, zeroing in on the smoking vehicle.

Opening the car door, Ben slid out, hands held high above his head. "I have three small children in the car, and my transmission's giving me trouble," he called. "We need a place to stay the night!"

The woman steadied the shotgun, her finger hovering near the trigger. She didn't flinch a muscle. "Are you here to get married?"

"No, ma'am! My car's acting up—it's the transmission."

The old woman hefted the gun higher, her eyes studying the situation. "Don't have many folks wanting to get married at this hour!"

"I don't want to get married!" Ben glanced helplessly at his sleeping kids. "Can you help us?" he shouted. The wind caught the car door and slammed it shut. Peg started from a sound sleep and burst into screams. Ben opened the door and leaned in to calm her.

He saw the old woman creep down the steps with the gun trained on him. The next thing he knew, a cold steel barrel rested at his temple.

"Easy," he murmured. Peg bawled harder, rousting Jody and Chris now.

A gravelly, masculine-sounding voice spoke ominously near to his ear. "How do I know you're not a criminal?"

"You don't, ma'am. And I am. I served eighteen months at Tipton, Missouri, for driving the getaway car for a friend during a convenience-store robbery. I was young and stupid. I had two young kids and a pregnant wife at home and I needed groceries and rent money. I served my time, and I was released early last month when my wife died a couple of days after a drunk driver hit her car. You have every right to send me back down the road, but I have to tell you I'll be on foot, and I'll be carrying three innocent kids on my back who had nothing to do with their dad's mistake—or with this weather."

The pressure of the barrel increased. "That's the biggest crock I've ever heard. Now get out of here." She pulled her hand back.

Ben straightened, meeting the woman's eyes. "It's

20

the honest truth, ma'am. I'll leave, but for the love of God, please let my children stay. They don't deserve to die in this storm." Snow whipped around them, snatching his words into the wind.

Ben never knew if it was the season—two days before Christmas—or the desperation in his voice that swayed Henrietta Humblesmith, but she studied him for a moment longer, then gradually lowered the gun and tramped around the car to the back passenger side, leaned in, and unhooked the strap to the car seat and lifted Peg into her arms.

Ben grabbed Jody and Chris and switched off the headlights. The two adults, carrying the sleepy children with a dog trotting behind, waded through deepening snowdrifts up to the house with the swaying sign:

THE MARRYING PARLOR
HENRIETTA HUMBLESMITH, PROPRIETOR
(CHRISTMAS VOWS: $5.00 EXTRA)

Henrietta Humblesmith (Ben discovered that really was her name) had fifteen rooms in the Marrying Parlor but only two with beds—Mrs. Humblesmith's and the guest room.

"The dog can stay on the service porch." She wrinkled her nose. "What's he rolled in?"

Ben shook his head. "I don't know, ma'am. He just joined the family about an hour ago."

The strange-looking woman wearing furry pink house shoes led the bedraggled followers up a set of winding wooden stairs and into a room on the left with a bed that had a metal headboard and an innerspring mattress. Warning Ben that she slept lightly—and with a gun—Henrietta left with two departing instructions: breakfast was on the table at six o'clock; bathroom was two doors down—and don't expect any heat upstairs.

Bedsprings creaked as Ben settled the kids between cold sheets; then he took off his jeans and crawled in beside them. Chris lay sideways, and Jody was already mumbling in her sleep. Peg rolled from stomach to back, sucking on an imaginary pacifier and occasionally crying out in her sleep. Ben knew he wasn't going to get much rest tonight, but at least they were out of the bad weather.

Beyond faded lace curtains the storm howled as Ben rolled to a fetal position, trying to still his chattering teeth. The heavy down comforter smelled of mothballs

and fabric softener. Tomorrow he'd get the old transmission patched and they'd make Mom's by nightfall. He'd sell the car and be on foot for a while, but those were the breaks.

"Thank you, God, for bringing me this far," he whispered, fighting back a swelling lump in his throat.

He didn't know anything about raising kids or being a decent dad. Sheila had borne the responsibility until now, but he did know that tonight he'd met an angel—okay, a bucktoothed, cranky one wielding a shotgun—but an angel, nevertheless, who had given him and his children shelter.

Right now, he figured he couldn't be picky about angels; he was just grateful God had sent one.

3

POPLAR BLUFF

MO

DECEMBER

Arctic sunlight streamed through the Marrying Parlor's elongated kitchen windows.

The storm had passed sometime near dawn. Snow lay in drifts against the porch, reminiscent of a Norman Rockwell picture. Oaks and junipers glistened with winter's best clothes.

Ben watched Henrietta spoon oatmeal into Peg's mouth, pausing between messy bites to coo baby talk to the child. The old woman was a fright in daylight: permanent-damaged red hair poking straight up through orange-juice-can curlers, skin so wrinkled it reminded Ben of an apple left in the bottom of the barrel for too long. The woman could eat lettuce through a venetian blind, Ben's gramps would have contended, but the lady had a heart of gold. Even Ben could see that in the brief time he'd been here. Her laugh was short and horsey sounding, but the underlying pleasure set off a ripple effect.

The kids loved Henrietta Humblesmith, and Ben figured kids had an edge on these things.

"Don't worry, Mom; we're all fine," Ben said, cradling the phone receiver between his neck and chin. "I'll get the transmission patched, and with any luck we'll make Poplar Bluff by late afternoon. . . . No, don't go to all that bother. I'll feed the kids before we get there." He mentally recalculated the peanut butter and hoped it would hold out. "The weather? Of course I'll drive careful, Mom. . . . I'm eating good." He winked at Henrietta. "Honest. . . . Sure, love you too. Now don't go to a lot of bother, you hear?"

He hung up the receiver and dropped into a kitchen chair. Henrietta jumped up and went to the stove. In a

few minutes she set a steaming plate of eggs and bacon before him. His stomach growled as the smell washed over him. He hadn't eaten a decent meal in days, reserving most of his portions for the children.

"I called collect," he assured the woman as he reached for the salt and pepper shakers. He'd pay Mom back when he got there.

Henrietta sat down and spooned the last of the cereal into the baby's mouth, then leaned over to butter Jody's toast. "Poor tykes. How long has their mommy been gone?"

"Couple of months." Ben had had a hard time dealing with Sheila's death at first, but then the gravity of what lay ahead temporarily overshadowed his grief. He had three kids to raise, three innocent lives that now depended on him, and God knew he'd let them down once before.

This time was going to be different. This time he had help.

He dug into the bacon and eggs, letting the salty, crisp meat and the tasty eggs linger on his palate. The eggs were fried the way he liked—whites nice and firm and the yolks oozing when he cut into them.

Reaching for the coffeepot, Henrietta topped off his cup. "Is it true?"

Ben glanced up, fork poised in midair. "Excuse me, ma'am?"

"The stuff you rattled on about last night. Is it true?"

Dropping his gaze, Ben sobered. "Every bit of it. I'm real grateful you allowed us to stay the night." He looked up, meeting her gaze solidly. "Why did you let us stay?"

She shrugged and sat down, biting into a piece of bacon. "I figured if you were honest enough to say what you did, you couldn't be all bad."

"I was stupid and desperate, and I let my family down," Ben said quietly.

The old woman's eyes appraised him. Ben supposed she was trying to decide if she could trust him. When she spoke, her voice sounded like ice in a blender, but underneath all that noise lurked a kind soul. "I don't condone crime, but sometimes desperation can make a man do crazy things." She reached for a piece of toast. "So you did some time in prison, did you?"

"Eighteen months."

She let out a low whistle, spreading jam on the bread.

28

Her eyes narrowed. "Must not have been your first offense."

"Oh, no, ma'am, it was my first offense."

The sentence had been harsh, but considering that a clerk had been hurt in the scuffle, the judge had shown no leniency. Ben didn't have the money to hire an attorney, so the court had appointed one—a young man who drank too much coffee and cried easily. The judge hadn't been swayed by male emotion, although the jury and Ben had been uncomfortable with the frequent outbursts. By the time the trial was over Ben had asked the judge to let him serve his time and put the incident behind him.

"Had a great-uncle who served time in Missouri once." Henrietta spooned sugar into her coffee thoughtfully. "When they let him out, they gave him a twenty-dollar gold piece, a Winchester rifle, and a mule."

Ben shook his head soberly. "They gave me a bus ticket."

"I'm getting a train for Christmas," Chris announced around a mouthful of cereal.

"You are!" Henrietta sat back, slapping both hands

on her knees. "Now that's a fine gift, all right. My boy got a train one Christmas. The little stink played with the box more than the toy."

"My train's going to have lots of tracks and houses and a whistle—a loud whistle," Chris contended.

"Is that the truth?" The old woman played along, pretending avid interest.

"Maybe Santa won't have an extra train this year, Chris." Ben tried to dampen the boy's expectation. He didn't have money for toy trains. There would be no train with a whistle under Mom's tree for Chris, and the boy was only going to be disappointed if he kept thinking this way.

"Uh-huh. I asked Santa and he said, 'Ho, ho, ho, have you been a good boy?' And I have been a good boy, so he said he'd see me on Christmas Eve. When is Christmas Eve, Daddy?"

Ben glanced at Henrietta. "Tonight, son."

"Oh, good! That's when Santa's gonna deliver my train. With lots of tracks and little houses and a—" he paused—"we're gonna be at Grandma's, so how will he find us?"

Ben nodded. "He'll find you."

"Whistle," Jody finished her brother's interrupted thought before taking a long drink of her milk.

"Yeah, a loud one."

"He's going to bring me a Fisher-Price toy kitchen," Jody said, primly wiping her mouth on a napkin. "A real neat one—with a oven that has a lightbulb in it."

The dog barked as a knock sounded on the back door. Heads pivoted to locate the early-morning visitor. A young couple trailing frosty breaths in the icy air stood on the porch, laughing up at each other. The young man reached out and rapped the windowpane sharply, his eyes riveted on the young lady.

"Oops," Henrietta said, shoving back from the table. "Got a customer." She shuffled across the floor, still wearing the red chenille robe and the pink flip-flops and those crazy orange-juice cans in her hair.

She opened the door with a wide grin spread across her homely features. She pushed the dog back with a slippered foot and waved the young couple inside. "Come in, come in!"

The couple sought the kitchen's warmth amid peals of excited laughter. Whipping off his hat, the gentleman announced that they were here to get married.

"No problem," Henrietta acquiesced. "Come with me." She glanced over her shoulder when she reached the doorway. "Ben, we'll be needing some witnesses. You and the kiddies come too."

Ben glanced at the couple anxiously. "Me?"

"It don't take a rocket scientist," Henrietta assured him. "Hurry along, or what's left of breakfast will be stone cold when we get back."

Hurriedly undoing the belt around the baby's waist, Ben lifted Peg from the makeshift high chair. Wiping Chris's and Jody's faces, he corralled the small entourage into the parlor.

Crepe-paper wedding bells dangled from the center light fixture, and a plastic rose-covered arch stood in the center of the room. An archaic pump organ sat to the left side, and five folding chairs lined the space in front of the podium.

Motioning for the participants to get into place, Henrietta sat down at the organ. "Any favorites?" she asked as her bulk established territory on the vinyl bench. The bride-to-be opened her mouth to respond, but Henrietta hit the first cord. "La, la la la," she bellowed. "Oh, promise me that someday you and Iiiiiiiiiiiiiiiii . . ."

The old organ wheezed and blew as Henrietta's gruff bass rattled the windows.

The young couple gazed adoringly into each other's eyes, oblivious to anything but each other and this moment.

With the last lines of the song, Henrietta slid off the bench. Her flip-flops slapped against the bare floor as she approached the plastic gardenia-bedecked podium. Clearing her throat, she focused on the nervous groom. "Let's see your license."

He fished in his pocket and produced the requested document. Henrietta scanned it and then cleared her throat, and the ceremony began.

Within minutes, the couple was pronounced man and wife, the new bride gleefully turning round and round, displaying the small, gold-encased diamond twinkling on her left hand. Henrietta handed Jody and Chris—to their utter delight—handfuls of rice to throw at the departing couple.

Balancing Peg on his hip, Ben signed the license on the witnesses line, adding the kids' names beneath his. "Is this legal?" he asked. He'd never heard of kids acting as witnesses.

"It's fine," Henrietta said. "Now help the kids throw the rice."

"How much?" the groom asked, eagerness to be on his way overshadowing thrift.

"Thirty dollars—vows during Christmas week are five dollars extra."

The man paid with a love-struck grin and, after downing a cup of eggnog, the couple, all smiles and giggles, departed in a flurry of rice pellets. The young man scooped up his bride halfway down the walk and carried her through deep snowdrifts the rest of the way to the car.

Ben and the children stood on the front porch beside Henrietta, waving until the silver Taurus slipped and slid back down the long snow-covered lane and eased onto the highway.

B en washed breakfast dishes and swept up crumbs,
then filled the ceramic sink with warm water and
gave Peg a bath.

She kicked and squealed, splashing water on the
worn linoleum and Ben. He was soaking wet when the
morning ritual was over and Peg was powder-dusted and
smelling sweet as a rose in clean clothes. He fastened her
back in the kitchen chair by tying the belt securely

around her waist and set some toys in front of her to keep her entertained.

"Homer Blott's got the only garage around," Henrietta told him when he turned his attention to the transmission. "He's pretty hard to get—always busy. Old Snood Grison's a pretty good shade-tree mechanic— always been able to fix anything I've taken him. I'll call Snood and ask if he can take a look at your problem. If he's not busy, he'll come right over."

Half an hour later, Snood Grison's '74 GMC pickup plowed up the drive, throwing snow over the fence line like a German tank, the heavy four-wheel drive eating up the rutted drifts.

The bandy-legged rooster of a man swung out of the truck seat, spitting a wad of tobacco juice over his shoulder, his deep-set eyes scanning the property. He took a moment to hitch up his faded denims before he started up the steep row of steps to the Marrying Parlor, whistling "Jingle Bells" off-key. Rapping on the front door, he stepped back to propel another wad of tobacco over the railing.

"Snood, as I live and breathe," Henrietta greeted, "get yourself in here!"

"Howdy, Henrietta!" All smiles, Snood whipped off a battered Stetson and breezed into the parlor. Introductions were made all around. Snood pinched little Jody's cheeks and fished around in his pockets until he found a peppermint for Chris. The children gaped wide-eyed at the funny-looking newcomer.

"Transmission actin' up on you?" he asked Ben.

"Bands are slipping and it's making a funny noise. I've lost first and second gears."

"Boy, that's a shame," Snood said. "Well, let's take a look."

The two men went outside while Henrietta kept the kids entertained beside the fire.

After disappearing under the Mercury for a time, Snood reappeared, shaking his head. "You got a problem."

Ben nodded. "Can you fix it, and do you know how much it will cost?"

"Well—" Snood dusted snow off his wool coat, his wizened features sobering—"yes and no. Yes, I can fix it and no, I don't know how much. Mercury parts around here are scarce as hen's teeth. If I can find parts at the junkyard it shouldn't be a bunch. If I have to order parts, then it could run anywheres between a hundred and a thousand bucks."

Ben's stomach pitched. "I don't have that kind of money."

The old man shook his head sympathetically. "Can you git it?"

"No, I'll have to sell the car and take the bus to Mom's."

How much did bus tickets for an adult and three kids cost? What would he do if they were more than two hundred eighty-nine dollars?

"Shame," Snood said. "Being so close to Christmas and all. Well, we won't borrow trouble—not when we have enough to see us through the day. Shucks, I'll call Homer and see if he can help. Then I'll tow your car on over to the garage. We'll git her fixed."

A little after ten, Henrietta fired up her Volks-wagen and backed out of the garage.

Ben loaded the kids and the car seat in the back and buckled himself into the front. A minute later the VW bug set off down the lane, plowing snow up to its head-lights.

The kids thought the outing was an adventure, but Ben thought it was the end of the line for the old

Mercury. He didn't have the money to fix the transmission, and they were wasting time looking for parts.

"Where does the bus stop around here?" He gripped the dashboard as the red bug shot out onto the deserted highway and spun its back tires. Smoke boiled out from under the chassis until rubber found traction. (Henrietta lacked something in the driving department.)

"Ed Wingate's filling station—but don't give up yet. Snood'll find those parts for you, or I'll bet a day's marrying pay."

The kids squealed with delight and bounced around in the backseat, pressing their noses to the side window glass. Snow drifted against fence posts, and tree branches hung heavy with their winter coats. The world looked like a giant ice-cream cone waiting for the first delectable lick.

The bug hummed along, eating up the snowy asphalt. "That's the beauty of these foreign jobs," Henrietta shouted above the din. "Dependable as daylight."

They stopped at Homer Blott's first, and he said they'd just have to look around. The closest junkyard was

in Eden, a small town eighteen miles to the east. Ben quickly discovered that used parts for a '73 Mercury weren't to be found there or anywhere. The VW crept up and down snowy drives and farm lanes all morning long without any luck. Toward noon, Henrietta treated the stranded family to hamburgers and fries at Ed's filling station, which also served as the town's bus stop, local café, and quick-grocery stop. By now Peg was cranky, needing a nap, and Jody and Chris were getting antsy from being confined to the backseat of the Volkswagen for the last three hours.

"You take the kiddies on home," Ed said. "I'll call around and see if I can hunt down some parts in Eden."

"Lucille!" Ed bellowed to his wife in the back room. "Bring these folks another order of fries. They've had a bad morning."

Ben shook his head. "I can't authorize you to buy the parts until I know how much—"

"Don't worry about money, son, we ain't found one part yet," Ed said. "Besides, it's Christmas." He eyed the fussy children and Ben, compassion alight in his eyes. "Things usually have a way of working out. *Lucille!* Where's those fries?"

Henrietta crammed the remainder of her burger into her mouth and reached for a napkin. "Haven't got time for more fries, Ed, but much obliged. Come on, Ben, let's get the kiddies home."

Ben shook hands with the man with the bladelike nose and then picked up Peg. She fussed, rubbing sleepy eyes.

The noisy group loaded back into the Volkswagen, and a few minutes later the bug shot out onto the highway, the kids' heads bobbling in the rear seat.

Ed Wingate's cheerful prediction rang in Ben's head on the slippery ride back to the Marrying Parlor. He wanted to believe life was that simple, that even the worst situations left hope, but he knew life was more complicated.

Christmas was tomorrow.

He had a few presents for the kids, but no money to fix the transmission. If it weren't for the mercy of Henrietta Humblesmith, he and his three kids would be living out of the car right now.

If he could only get to Poplar Bluff and Mom, then the kids might have a decent holiday. Presents would be scarce, but Mom always had a little something wrapped

and under the tree. The house would be full of Christmas smells—of fresh sprigs of holly and of turkey roasting in the oven. He thought about the wooden bowl Mom kept in the center of the dining-room table year-round. It would be brimming with nuts and apples and oranges this time of year—and a nutcracker. That particular tool used to fascinate Ben. He'd sit for hours cracking walnuts and picking out the firm meat. Mom used the nuts in candy and cookies; Ben could still taste the divinity and walnut balls. But if he couldn't get the car running, his children wouldn't be cracking walnuts. They wouldn't have a Christmas, however small.

They would be sitting in Henrietta Humblesmith's parlor witnessing wedding vows performed by an eccentric woman wearing a red housecoat and pink somethings on her feet and orange-juice cans in her hair.

He still thought children witnessing wedding vows might be illegal. What had she done for witnesses before he and the children came along?

A thin sun spared the afternoon from a bone-rattling chill. Shortly after they got back to the Marrying Parlor, Henrietta said she was worn out and she was going to take a short nap.

Peg had catnapped on the drive home from Homer Blott's garage so, revived by food and sleep, she was raring to go. Jody and Chris considered the word *nap* tantamount to social treason and vowed they weren't sleepy. That left Ben to entertain three kids and a dog for a couple of hours in a strange environment. Buttoning the children's hoods tightly, he herded them outside to play.

Towering cumulus clouds skittered across patches of turquoise blue sky. Sunlight bounced off glistening snow piles, and Ben slipped on a pair of sunglasses to combat the glare.

"Look, Daddy!" Jody pointed to a cloud formation suspended high overhead. "An elephant!"

Sure enough, the cloud looked exactly like an elephant with a long trunk pointing to the east. Jabbering, Peg pointed to the cloud and grinned.

Once the children had their fill of the fun sight, they waded through deep drifts, snow covering their ratty boots.

"I'll walk ahead, and you follow in my footsteps," Ben told the bright-eyed, teeth-chattering elves.

Ben draped Peg's legs around his neck and carried her on his shoulders as she babbled, pointing at the sky, at her hair, and at her eyes, talking gibberish but openly in favor of the excursion.

"I'm cold, Daddy." Chris huddled deeper into his

46

coat, a light wind whipping the tip of his nose and turning it bright red.

Jody was prissier—and more practical. "I'm getting
all wet." Her shoes were already showing signs of damp-
ness.

Ben ignored the rumblings, determined to make the
outing brief but fun. They tramped over the hillside,
crawling under fences and skimming cattle guards when
Jody vowed for certain she'd fall through the steel cracks.

Wildlife cavorted in the fresh snowfall, scampering
to safety when the noisy troop approached. A white-
tailed rabbit bounded across the path, evoking delighted
giggles out of Peg. Dog raced about, barking and chasing
unsuspecting game.

"Chris, when we get to Grandma's I'm going to
show you a picture of a dog that I owned when I was a
kid," Ben called.

Old Rattler was a hound—the best hunting dog in
Boone County. Ben remembered the weekends he'd
spent on the farm with Grandma and Grandpa. Grandpa used to take him hunting early mornings. They rarely
shot anything, and anything they did bag they'd bring
home and Grandma cooked it with biscuits and gravy

at noon. Ben never forgot the thrill of those outings. He supposed it was one of those "man things" Sheila used to tease him about, but he wanted Chris to experience his share of memories. He wanted so much more for his kids than he was able to give, but memories he could provide.

Henrietta's property line extended for twenty acres, so Ben knew he had plenty of room to explore.

"Look, Daddy!" Jody bent to pick up an acorn poking up through a drift. A moment later Chris found a second nut. Ben paused, staring up, up, up to the very top of a massive oak. The tree had been loaded with nuts, enough ammunition to supply a good nut fight.

The hunt was on as the two older children scurried about in the deep drifts, gathering nuts and storing the treasures in their coat pockets. Dog raced about, yapping and tripping Jody twice. Peg squealed, cupping her pudgy hand in quest of her own treat.

Ben reached down and scooped up a handful of acorns, sticking them jauntily in the baby's hood and coat pockets. The little girl giggled, her nose chaffed red in the cold air.

"Look at us, Daddy!" Chris and Jody planted their

snow-covered boots in their father's footsteps, showing off bulging coat pockets comically distorted with acorns. Jumping up and down, Jody dislodged the nuts and sent them popping out of her pockets in every direction.

Chris followed suit, and their nutty antics had Ben on his knees, laughing.

Peg balanced precariously on his shoulder, clinging to his upraised coat sleeve in wide-eyed awe, bursting into an overturned giggle box of chortles when the nuts continued to fly out.

Dropping into a snowbank, Ben set Peg aside and spread his arms wide, flapping like a bird. "Caw, caw!" he yelled.

"Caw, caw, caw." His words echoed over the quiet hillside.

The kids stopped jumping and stared at him.

"Caw!"

"Caw, caw, caw."

Ben watched the girls from beneath lowered lids. Peg's cornflower blue eyes were large and round; Jody's expression implied she didn't know if he was hurt, playing, or just plain crazy.

He slowly pivoted his head, meeting his daughters' rapt gazes. Lifting a knitted brow, he said, "Caw."

Chris caught onto the game and dove on top of Ben, heaping handfuls of snow on his dad's chest. Peg got into the act, her baby hands flinging snow while the wind sent the wet, white powder back in her face.

Blinking wetness away, she giggled.

A wrestling match ensued; even Dog joined the fun, tugging at Ben's coat sleeve until finally Ben had to throw in the towel. "Okay, line up! We're going to make snow angels."

The kids assumed positions in the snow, and the game began.

"Look at me, Daddy! I'm making an angel!"

"Do angels have feet, Daddy? Real feet?"

Dog made a run for a snow pile and slid comically on his belly.

Peg jabbered, kicking snow into her eyes with her thrashing feet.

When the angels were complete, a snowball fight broke out. Jody gave up quickly, but Chris and Ben fought it out until Ben threw his hands up in mock surrender. Thoughts turned to building a snow wall that extended across the path and blocked all furry wildlife intruders.

Thirty minutes later the happy troop moved on, leaving behind one large angelic form flanked on either side by two smaller ones—and a slightly messy but nevertheless significant infant angelic imprint—in the pristine snow. Before they left, Ben took a stick and wrote each of their names in front of the heavenly silhouettes.

CHRISTOPHER
JOLEEN
PEG
DADDY

Then in big letters underneath, he wrote:

THE O'KEEFES WISH YOU
A BLESSED CHRISTMAS AND
A HAPPY NEW YEAR

The message stretched over the silver pasture so that any small aircraft flying over would see the holiday greeting.

Size eleven footprints forged the way, and four struggling smaller feet hurried to keep up.

A few minutes later the prints returned to the angels. Ben managed to corral Dog long enough to make four paw prints beside the angel forms. Then with the same stick he wrote:

DOG

*C*louds *began to fill in, but weather seemed the least of the kids' concerns.*

Ben realized their shoes were soaking wet now. He determined to turn around, but the kids raced back and forth on the forged path, looking at the animal tracks in the snow and guessing which kind of animal made them. Chris found an empty bird's nest. Eyes bright with excitement, he brought the find to Ben, who explained that it probably belonged to a wren who had raised several families that summer. The boy carried the prize as carefully as if he were handling nuclear waste, walking so deliberately that Ben wondered if they'd make it back to Henrietta's by nightfall.

Jody poked a stick into drifts along the path, pausing to scoop away the fresh snow and discover more delights: fall leaves—burnished rust of oaks, golden birch, and crimson maples.

Gathering a handful, the child carefully arranged them in a wet pile and entrusted the foliage to Ben. "Nana's Christmas presents," she announced proudly.

Ben carried the trophies for the remainder of the outing.

Ahead, a gurgling stream zigzagged through the property line. Holding his hand up for silence, Ben spotted a doe and her fawn drinking from the icy water.

Her head went up, and she paused, alert, as the wind carried their scent.

Jody eased closer to Ben. "Look, it's a momma deer."

Nodding, Ben knelt and cautioned the kids to keep quiet. "We'll scare her off."

Eyes alert, the deer assessed the danger from a distance.

"She's so pretty," Jody whispered.

"She sure is." Ben studied the peaceful scene, mother and baby drinking from life-giving waters. Peace washed over him, a peace he hadn't felt in a very long time, certainly one missing since Sheila's death. They'd had their ups and downs, but love had always been strong between them. Her death had wasted away Ben's heart, as sure as an incurable disease.

"The mommy deer is taking care of the baby deer," Jody explained to Chris in a hushed whisper. "Like Mommy used to take care of us, huh, Daddy?"

Tears smarted Ben's eyes, and he turned away from the sight. He'd missed eighteen months of his kids' life, eighteen months more he could have had with Sheila. The morning Ben was sentenced Sheila had been told they were expecting a baby. Sheila had kept his picture on the kitchen table and talked about him every day to Jody and Chris—and Peg, when she was born. He'd taped pictures of Sheila and the three kids next to his bunk. Sheila, Chris, Jody, and the baby were the last thing he would see before he closed his eyes at night and the first thing he saw when he opened them each morning.

Were it not for God's grace and Sheila, he wouldn't have made it through the past eighteen months. Hot tears rolled down his cheeks and dripped off the tip of his chin as he tightened his hold on Peg.

A small, gloved hand curled around his neck, and Jody rested her icy cheek against his. "When she was in the 'mergency room after the accident, Mommy said when I saw you crying I'm s'posed to tell you something."

Emotion was so tight in Ben's throat he could hardly speak past the knot. "What's that, sweetheart?"

"Mommy said when you cried—and she said you'd probably do that a lot for a while—I'm s'posed to tell you that she loves you very much, and someday you'll be together in heaven. That's where Mommy is, Daddy. In heaven, with Jesus, so we shouldn't be sad because she can't be with us." Tears competed with wisdom in the child's turquoise eyes. "But I miss her so much, and I feel like crying too, sometimes, but I don't 'cause I have to be a big girl and help you. Right, Daddy?"

Patting the cherubic hand, Ben shook his head, too overcome to speak.

"We can make it if we stick together." Jody's arm tightened around his neck. Chris eased closer, his eyes openly showing support.

"And," Jody continued, whispering into Ben's right ear now, "Mommy said when I grow up and get married I'm s'posed to look for a man just like you, Daddy, 'cause you're good to the bone."

Good to the bone. Sheila's voice echoed through Jody's.

"Thank you, sweetheart." Ben squeezed his daughter's arm and then wiped tears on his jacket sleeve to clear his vision.

Thank you, Sheila.

Splendid fingers of red and gold spread across the western sky as Ben and the three kids ended the treasure hunt and trudged slowly back to the Marrying Parlor. They were numb with cold, and the kids' feet were soaking wet despite the old boots. Ben prayed they wouldn't get sick; he didn't have money for a doctor bill or medicine. But it had been a good afternoon—a priceless few

hours money couldn't buy. The kids' pockets were full of nuts and feathers and burnished gold leaves found beneath the snow.

And their hearts were full of memories.

Memories of watching a doe and her fawn drink from a stream surrounded by God's majestic beauty; making snow angels together; a wife's heartfelt assurances passed on through the mouth of her child: "You're good to the bone, Daddy."

And for Ben, the best of all: a young wife's promise from the grave: "We'll be together again someday."

His heart felt full for the first time in years.

A green Cadillac with a set of longhorns welded to the front grill sat in front of the Marrying Parlor when Ben and the kids climbed the front porch steps.

The sound of organ music drifted from beneath closed doors. Ben figured a wedding service was going on.

Stomping snow off his boots, he herded the kids inside and told them to run upstairs and change their wet clothes, and he'd be along in a few minutes. Peg was thirsty, jabbering and pointing toward the kitchen. Before he could see to the child's needs, the parlor doors swung open and Henrietta appeared, her horsey laugh filling the entryway.

"Been waiting for you to get back—come on in! Got a couple of folks here who need a witness."

For the second time that day, Ben and Peg were present for marriage nuptials, those of Harold Dean Dawson and Fayrene Michelle Farnsworth, both hailing from Houston, Texas.

The eccentric, big, beefy Texan wore a cowboy hat, a western suit, and a pair of black ostrich boots. His million-dollar smile lit up the room.

"Thank you, son, thank you," he boomed, pressing a hundred-dollar bill in Ben's hand when the vows were complete. Bending closer and giving Ben a sly wink, he whispered, "Take this and buy your little girl something pretty."

Ben tried to hand the bill back, protesting, "I didn't do anything other than stand here."

The merry bridegroom grinned, giving Ben a jovial slap on the back. "It's Christmas, boy! I got me the pret-

tiest little filly this side of Houston and more money than Quaker has got oats. Enjoy, boy, enjoy!"

Henrietta served eggnog. After gulping down a cup, the jolly Texan winked at his bride, and the happy newlyweds made a quick exit for the door.

Ben glanced at Henrietta, and she gave another belly horselaugh. "I love these lovesick people. They just make my day."

Lifting a brow, Ben watched the old woman shuffle toward the kitchen, mumbling something under her breath about having the best job in the world and don't anybody tell her any different.

His eyes returned to the crisp one-hundred-dollar bill in his hand. He couldn't believe it. One hundred dollars—for watching two people say less than a half-dozen words. One hundred dollars—enough to pay for bands and a pump for the car, maybe, if he was lucky.

The aroma of bubbling spices drifted from the stove and filled the old house with mouthwatering smells. The parlor glittered with Christmas finery, but Ben noticed the living room bore no signs of celebration. No garland or pine or flashing red and green lights to mark the holiday.

Henrietta returned momentarily, her fuzzy slippers slapping against hardwood.

"Where are the other young'uns?" She set a bowl of oranges, apples, and nuts on the dining-room table, helping herself to a nut.

"Changing clothes—they got a little wet."

"That's what kids do." She cracked the nut and fished the meat out of the shell, then popped it into her mouth. "You look a might worn out. Why don't you leave Peg and the other two with me and you go upstairs and catch a little nap before supper?"

A nap? Ben's bones ached for uninterrupted sleep; he'd had little since getting out of prison. Peg was usually up two or three times a night looking for Sheila. Ben couldn't remember the last time he'd had a nap.

"I couldn't let you do that, Henrietta—"

"Nonsense." The woman reached for Peg, urging Ben toward the stairway. "Power nap, isn't that what they call it these days? Go on now, take advantage of my good nature." She grinned, grabbing the baby's fist and pretending to gobble it up. "We're going to give that stinky-smelling dog a bath and let him dry by the fire, aren't we, sweetums?"

Jody and Chris clunked down the stairs dressed in dry clothing. Chris had his shirt on wrong side out, and both were wearing their good shoes.

Henrietta adjusted Chris's clothing, clucking under her tongue. "You're just in time," she told the two older kids with a wink. "I need some help bathing a dog and making cookies."

"Cookies!" Chris's eyes brightened. The kids trailed Henrietta into the kitchen, chattering a mile a minute.

Ben was suddenly left with nothing to do but take a late-afternoon nap. Settling onto the old mattress, he thanked God for Henrietta Humblesmith and promptly fell asleep a minute after his head hit the pillow.

Delicious smells wafted from the oven as Henrietta and Jody rolled out cookie dough and cut various shapes: bells, wreaths, stars, and snowmen. Dog lay by the stove in the living room, drying off from his bath.

Christmas wreaths and stars baked to a golden brown in the oven, the smell of baking cookies scenting the kitchen and the heat from the oven frosting the windowpanes. Peg sat in her makeshift high chair, eating the treats almost as fast as Henrietta could pull them out of the oven. Chris sat at the table with a dishcloth tied around his neck, manning the icing section. He smeared red and green on the cool cookies and sprinkled them with multicolored sparkles and beaded toppings. Icing dotted every inch of the tabletop, and Henrietta knew if she were to walk over to the table she'd be stepping in sprinkles and sparkles. Land, what a mess kids could make—but what a welcome one.

There'd be no supper for the O'Keefe kids tonight because she'd ruined it, but Henrietta figured Christmas Eve was special and a body had a right to spoil their supper one day of the year.

Cleaning the icing off Peg, the old woman untied the belt and lifted the child out of the chair. She sat down with her in the old rocker next to the window, calling for the other two to come closer.

Still licking a spoon, Chris joined her and Jody followed. Pulling a child's storybook from a stack of magazines, Henrietta patted her knee and invited the older two to climb aboard. The children—all three now—sat in her lap, their childlike smell filling her senses. Closing

her eyes, she savored the almost forgotten scent. Wind and the outdoors and soft, powdered-sugar breath.

Opening the book, Henrietta read: "And it came to pass there were shepherds watching their flock in the fields."

Jody knew the Christmas story well, repeating many of the words in unison with Henrietta as she read the account from the children's book of the Savior's birth in Bethlehem over two thousand years ago.

Henrietta sighed contentedly. Kiddies made Christmas. Without them, the house would be empty as a tomb tonight. Her mind stretched back to the years her own children's laughter had filled these big rooms. Her eyes misted as she remembered days gone by.

Christmas was never the same when family was grown. Her daughter, Beth, lived in California and hadn't been home in fifteen years; Paul was busy with his own family in Wyoming. He called occasionally, but something always prevented a holiday visit. Gaily wrapped packages and cards accompanied their letters of regret. The kids always sent a pretty Christmas card that said something like "Thinking of you though we're

miles apart." Then scrawled below: "Love you, Mom. Have a great Christmas!"

But cards couldn't replace smiles in person.

And they sure couldn't take the place of a mother holding her child in her arms after so many years.

A year ago Henrietta had gotten tired of the excuses and her loneliness and decided to open a Marrying Parlor. What a difference that decision made in her life! Nearly every day—and at least twice a week in the off-season—couples drove up the lane and knocked on her door. Sometimes they were accompanied by witnesses, sometimes not. It didn't matter to Henrietta. The looks on those folks' faces when she pronounced them man and wife was worth a million dollars. But truth be known, Henrietta would have performed the nuptials for nothing, except for Christmas vows.

Christmas vows were five dollars extra.

She had something to look forward to these days—all because of her new business.

Henrietta could have filled her time with clubs and church activities, but she didn't take to organized religion. She knew the Lord and served him in her own way.

Some might frown on her methods, but then she would be the one to stand in front of the Father on Judgment Day and explain her actions. She sent the five dollars extra for Christmas vows to Norman A. Prudwell, pastor of the Methodist church about a mile down the road (she got his name off the sign in front of the clapboard church). She always included a note saying, "Put the money in the collection plate on Christmas morning."

A handsome gift for the Christ child on his birthday. It was a real shame how some folks plain forgot to give the Honoree his present. People rushed here and there, buying for everyone but the guest. Henrietta took her marrying earnings and put them in a holly-embossed envelope—was even known to occasionally drop it in the plate herself (though not often).

"Happy birthday, Lord," she'd say under her breath, and feel real good about the process.

Tonight was Christmas Eve, and she had a feeling she might ought to deliver the gift herself, seeing as how . . .

Sighing, the old woman turned the page and continued reading to a sleepy Peg. The other children's heads rested peacefully against her bosom, their eyes droopy from the kitchen's warmth, their faces smeared with Christmas goodies.

Henrietta knew it was going to be an extra special Christmas this year, thanks to Ben O'Keefe and his family.

An extra special one.

After supper the phone rang.

Snood Grison's voice came over the line. "Good news and bad news, son."

"Give me the bad news first," Ben said. Since good news was scarce as hen's teeth lately, he didn't figure it was going to improve now.

"Homer Blott and I've located the parts, but it's going to be the day after Christmas before we can get your car fixed. Homer and his boy, Lonnie, they got a rush job that Homer's promised one of his regular customers, and they won't finish up until late tonight. Tomorrow being Christmas and all, he's got to let Lonnie off because he's got four kids and a wife—but Homer promised they'll get to work on your car day after Christmas."

Ben closed his eyes, feeling sick. What should he do now? He couldn't impose on Henrietta's hospitality for another two days. Mom would be disappointed that the kids wouldn't be there for Christmas. Money had been so tight Sheila hadn't been able to make the trip to Poplar Bluff while he was in jail. Mom was counting on having Ben and the kids home for the first time in years. Last Christmas, Sheila had written Ben and said she'd sent Thelma a new Mr. Coffee, and Mom had called Christmas night to thank her.

Sure sorry, Mom; it looks like it's going to be another Mr. Coffee year. Only this year, Ben had bought her a box of handkerchiefs with her name embroidered in pink.

"I think I'd like to hear the good news now."

"Homer says he'll give you credit."

Ben had learned long ago not to fight Murphy's Law. The harder you fought, the worse it got. "If that's the best we can do."

"Homer says if you'll help, he'll even knock off a little for labor. You know anything about pulling a transmission?"

"I'm pretty good with my hands—worked in a garage one summer." Ben frowned. "I'd be real grateful if I could help and knock down the cost of repairs."

"Then come over to Blott's Garage now, and I'll help you get the old transmission out so we can be ready to slip the new parts in Tuesday morning. Henrietta will drive you over and bring the kiddies. The garage is warm—Homer built a woodstove that'll peel the paint off the wall. The kids can't hurt a thing."

So Henrietta and Ben and the kids bundled up and piled into Henrietta's car. With Henrietta at the wheel, the Volkswagen plowed snow up to its headlights driving down the lane. The kids bounced around in the backseat, excited about yet another new adventure.

It was colder than a dead man's tongue tonight, the wind whipping through the bare trees and across

the snow-covered landscape. Drifts piled against fence posts and a cold moon hung overhead.

Jody dangled over the backseat near Ben's right ear. "What if Santa Claus can't find us, Daddy? I told God where we were last night, but I didn't tell Santa."

"Santa knows where you are, sweetie."

"But what if he forgets?" Chris jumped into the conversation, concern coloring his tone. "We're not even at Grandma's house. He'll be looking for us, and he's got a lot of kids to look for."

"He'll find you," Ben assured in a soothing tone.

Ben thought about the three small packages in the Mercury trunk: a Barbie doll for Jody, a box of miniature cars—twenty in all—for Chris. A set of Fisher-Price tub toys for Peg. Forty-five dollars' worth of Wal-Mart Christmas, all the money he had managed to save for eighteen months; but he was thankful the Lord had supplied that. That's all his kids would have this year: forty-five dollars' worth of toys and a whole lot of love.

He thought about the crisp one-hundred-dollar bill in his pocket and quickly dismissed the idea of another shopping trip. The money was a godsend; if he were fortunate, it would be enough to cover the garage bill.

"I'm still a little worried." Jody peered at him, her angelic face illuminated by the dash lights. "Are you sure he'll find us?"

Henrietta chuckled. "He's right smart for his age, honey. He'll find you. Chris, honey, get the dog out of my face. He's getting slobbers on my coat."

The children seemed satisfied with the reassurances.

Henrietta reached the highway, and the little bug fishtailed onto the road.

Traffic was light tonight. Ben figured most folks were gathering for church services and family dinners; after all, it was Christmas Eve. Henrietta hadn't mentioned church, so Ben didn't know her beliefs, but she had a lot of pictures on the wall, with sayings like "Knock and the door will be opened," and she had this knitted thing made of white yarn hanging above the stove, and if you stared at it long enough, the words *Jesus Saves* materialized. She seemed like a kind soul, a lady who enjoyed her work. Ben noticed how her face lit up every time she pronounced a man and woman husband and wife. She'd take the bride's and groom's hands and join them together, saying in that coarse voice of hers, "What God has joined together let no

man separate—and that means divorce lawyers, you hear me, young'uns?" Ben guessed she must believe in a higher power.

Up ahead, cars were pulling into the Methodist church parking lot, folks getting out of their cars and calling holiday greetings to each other.

"Christmas Eve Communion service," Henrietta observed.

Ben watched the church getting closer, wishing he could attend. He and Mom had planned to take the kids to church tonight, then open presents later.

The Volkswagen puttered down the highway, its taillights twinkling in the blackness. The old woman slid a sidelong glance in Ben's direction. "Don't attend church on a regular basis. How about you?"

"Yes, ma'am—I went every Sunday in prison. Plan to keep it up once I get settled."

They were there now, in front of the picturesque sanctuary. Warm light streamed from the lead glass windows, forming a colorful symmetrical pattern in the snow. The kids pressed noses against the side windows, their eyes following the holiday activity.

Patting her coat pocket, Henrietta said quietly.

"Don't suppose Homer would mind if we stop off and take Communion. It *is* Christmas Eve."

"No, ma'am. Don't suppose he would," Ben said, grinning.

"What about Dog?" Chris asked. "Can he go inside with us?"

The mutt tilted his head, one ear lolling to the side.

"He'll have to stay in the car, hon. I'll leave the motor running so he won't get cold. These bugs don't burn hardly any gas."

Inside the church the wooden pews filled quickly. The small building couldn't hold over fifty people. According to the tally board hanging behind the choir loft they'd taken in $123.36 in last Sunday's offering. The congregation numbered eighty-nine; forty-three had been in attendance last Lord's Day.

Locating seats near the front, Henrietta, Ben, and the children sat down. Candles flickered on the altar table, the scent of pine permeating the air.

Pastor Norman A. Prudwell entered from a side door, and the gathering swelled to its feet. The strains of "Silent Night" filled the old church as two young girls wearing white robes and crowns of thistle came slowly down the aisle, bearing long, golden poles with fire on the end. After touching the wicks to the altar candles, they extinguished the pole flames and took their seats on the front pew.

Ben's deep baritone blended with Henrietta's gruff contralto as they lifted their voices in songs of praise. When the offering plate came by, Ben dropped in a twenty-dollar bill—20 percent of the unexpected hundred-dollar gift.

Henrietta Humblesmith carefully placed a holly-festooned envelope into the plate, briefly closing her eyes in what looked to Ben like a silent prayer.

Pastor Prudwell read from the second chapter of Luke before the children of the church put on a small play depicting Mary, Joseph, the baby Jesus, and the three wise men from the East.

Chris and Jody rocked with laughter (along with the congregation, except for the participant's mother) when one of the wise men tripped on the hem of his robe and took a swift, headlong plunge into the manger, spared from imminent disgrace at the last moment by a quick-thinking Joseph.

Then the holiest of holies took place: the breaking of

bread and drinking of the ceremonial wine. Hands lifted to accept the elements symbolizing the broken body of Christ and the Savior's shed blood. Faces glowed with accepted love and reverent gratitude, as they ate and drank the elements in celebration of the birth of the Christ child.

Closing his eyes, Ben held tightly to his children's hands. In his heart, Sheila stood beside him. On this most holy night of the year, Ben O'Keefe praised a living God.

B lott's Garage sat off the highway at the junction of
EE and Old Line Road, a good three miles away
from the Marrying Parlor.

The VW pulled in, and Ben unfastened the car
seat and pulled Peg's stocking cap snugly over her
ears. Wind buffeted the group as they dashed for the
set of double doors. Henrietta knocked once, and the
door slowly lifted. The newcomers hurried inside to

the warmth of a potbellied woodstove standing in the middle of the oil-stained concrete floor. *Snood Grison is right,* Ben thought. *That black monstrosity puts out enough heat to supply hell with a direct pipeline.*

"We were getting worried about you," Homer hollered from beneath the back of a jacked-up pickup. "Thought you might have gotten stuck in a snowdrift."

"We stopped off for church services," Henrietta said.

Metal tires screeched as Homer pushed the creeper clear of the vehicle to peer up at the ceiling as if it were about to cave in on him.

"I go to church," the old woman snapped in response to his teasing. She sniffed. "Occasionally."

Within minutes, the kids stripped off coats and gloves, their eyes wide with curiosity as they explored the new surroundings. Ben's eyes scanned the metal building. An older model pickup, maybe a GMC, dominated the pit area. The smell of grease hung in the overheated room. Homer Blott, the owner, was dressed in a pair of oil-covered overalls.

Homer rolled back under the truck, and his muffled

voice asked, "Where you been keeping yourself these days, Henrietta?"

"Been real busy, Homer. Married fourteen couples this month alone. This here is Ben O'Keefe—the one with the transmission problems? He's trying to make it to his mother's in Poplar Bluff for the holidays."

Homer wheeled out from under the truck again, stood up, and began wiping his greasy hands on a shop rag. Extending a somewhat cleaner hand, he smiled. "Merry Christmas, Ben. This here is my boy, Lonnie."

Lonnie grinned, shaking hands with Ben. "Howdy."

Ben nodded. "Merry Christmas."

The older Blott turned to view the kids. "And these must be your young'uns?"

"Yes, sir—Jody, Chris, and little Peg." Ben grinned at his youngest. "And that's Dog, over there."

Homer turned to look at the mutt. "Dog?"

"We haven't named him yet."

Peg's eyes fixed on the small tree brightly twinkling on the workbench. Branches were decorated in red and green lights, and paper chains adorned the tree.

"Guess Snood told you I can fix you right up, but it's going to be day after tomorrow before we can get to it,"

Homer said. "Awful sorry, but I promised Hague Trotter I'd have his truck back to him late tonight. Then with Christmas tomorrow—"

Ben smiled. "I understand, sir. I appreciate the help."

"Shame to have troubles here at Christmas." Homer's eyes skimmed the kiddies sympathetically.

If Ben's troubles were confined only to Christmas, he'd have been grateful. The commercial aspect of the holiday didn't mean much to him; but the Savior's birth was real special. Presents, turkey, and dressing with all the trimmings had been absent from his life for a while now. Chris's eyes, bright with expectation, were on the tree. Jody and Peg would get a doll and some tub toys, respectively, but he'd wanted to give them so much more this year.

God, I'm a failure. I failed Sheila, and I'm going to fail the kids this Christmas, and sometimes—no, often—I fail you. I'm sorry, Lord. Help me to do better.

Henrietta turned to greet Homer's wife as she came through the back door. "Why, Maxine, I wondered where you were."

The stout, pint-sized woman wearing a man's over-

coat unwrapped a thick wool scarf and pulled it off a head of snow-white hair. "Henrietta, where you been keeping yourself these days?"

"Been busier than a one-armed wallpaper hanger, Maxine." Henrietta leaned over to give Jody a maternal hug. "Got visitors this Christmas Eve. This here is little Jody, and over there are Chris and Peg. Transmission's going out of their daddy's car, and Homer's going to fix it."

Maxine flashed a sunny smile. "Well, looks like the menfolk have their hands full. Why don't you and the girls come inside the house? You can watch me make stuffing and clean the turkey and we'll have us a good old-fashioned hen party."

Jody glanced expectantly to Ben for confirmation. He nodded. "Mind your manners."

Peg went into Henrietta's waiting arms, and the womenfolk left the garage in a flurry of female chattering.

The overhead door rattled open and Snood Grison stomped into the building, his breath trailing a frosty vapor. Dog shot over to investigate the new arrival.

Nose bright as a cherry, eyes sparkling with

mischief, Snood yelled, "Ho, ho, ho," and gravitated to the workbench. In his arms he carried a bundle of shiny yellow pine. The spicy smell of new lumber overrode the smell of grease as he set the stack of wood on the bench and briskly warmed his hands by the fire.

"What's that?" Chris asked, stepping closer to peer around the old man's shoulders.

Snood grinned. "Why, that's Christmas, son. I'm about to make my grandson's present." He paused, giving the lad a sly wink. "Say, I could sure use some help—think you could hand me tools?"

Chris beamed, looking to Ben for permission.

"Go on," Ben encouraged, easing the boy closer to the bench. Snood stepped back from the fire to arrange the lumber and lay a sack of nails and a hammer in the work area.

Overcome by shyness, Chris continued to hang back.

"Ever owned a rabbit trap, son?"

Ben doubted that Chris knew anything about the contraption. He had never taken his son hunting or fishing or, for that matter, done anything normal fathers and sons shared.

Chris shook his head, refusing to meet Grison's eyes.

"Well, don't worry. I'll teach you everything you need to know."

Positioning a six-foot strip of pine, he reached for a circular saw and flipped the switch. "We're going to make two boxes, each six inches high, ten inches wide, and twenty-eight inches long."

Chris threw his hands over his ears as the blade sheared through the pine, kicking up flakes of shavings.

While Homer and his son, Lonnie, worked beneath the pickup, Snood measured, hammered, and sawed. Chris handed him nails and quickly confiscated pieces of wooden scraps Grison heaped in a pile. Christmas carols blared from a white GE radio with a jagged crack running up the side, perched high above the workbench.

"Do people keep the rabbits they catch?" Chris asked, eyes glued to the work in progress.

"Don't think that'd be wise, son. The kind of rabbit you'd catch in this trap is used to being on his own—he wouldn't like being kept in a cage."

"Then why even bother him?"

The men, no longer underneath the truck, paused in their pursuits to exchange looks. The voice of Burl

Ives drifted from the radio, singing "Frosty the Snow-man."

After a moment, Snood cleared his throat. "Well, some folks like to catch them for sport. Like my grand-boy, Skip. Now Skipper catches and releases—do you understand what that means?"

Chris shook his head.

"Means you catch the rabbit, then set him free." Snood turned back to the workbench and fastened a hook on the door of each trap. Chris crowded closer. "Now you see, son, this is how it works. You prop this slot open, and you bait the trap with a carrot, apple, or grain—whatever you like. The trapdoor slides down through the slot to close off when the rabbit trips the catch."

Chris leaned in close, peering intently. "What's that stick in the middle?"

"That's what the rabbit trips to close the door."

"Cool."

Snood stepped back, admiring his work. Two fine-looking traps sat on the bench, waiting for gift tags.

Rummaging in a brown sack, the old man took out a

couple of red bows and handed them to Chris. "This looks like a job for your department."

The child stuck the sticky side of a bow to the first trap, his eyes bright with excitement. Ben stood back and grinned. He'd never seen the boy so animated. Sheila had done the best she could raising the kids alone, but Ben guessed there'd been few times in Chris's life, if any, that he'd had the fun of building something from scratch. Sheila's stepdad was a trucker and on the road most of the time, and Ben's dad had died when Ben was nine. Ben's kids didn't have a grandpa who made rabbit traps or handed out peppermints from his coat pocket.

Chris fastened the second bow in place and then stood back, grinning. The traps made a splendid sight with red bows and shiny new pine set off by the background of the tiny blinking Christmas tree.

"Look, Daddy! I helped make a rabbit trap!" Chris exclaimed.

"Well, you sure did—and mighty nice-looking traps, Chris!"

Chris beamed under Ben's approval. Dog came around to inspect, sniffing the red bows.

After rummaging a few more minutes, Snood

produced a couple of wrinkled gift tags. Reaching for the pencil stuck behind his ear, he laid the tags on the workbench and mused aloud. "Let's see . . . this one's for Skipper from Grandpa." He handed the tag to Chris. "Stick it next to the bow."

When the boy finished, he raced back to the workbench.

"Okay, now this one . . ." Pausing, Snood whipped off his hat and scratched a thatch of thinning hair, mischief twinkling in his coin-shaped eyes. "Now let me think . . . can't recall who I made this one for. . . ."

Chris watched, eyes intent on Snood's every move.

"Oh sure, I remember now." The old man bent and scribbled something on the second tag, then held it out at arm's length and read what he had written: "'To Chris, from his new friend, Snood.'"

Chris's jaw dropped. "Me, Chris?"

Old Man Grison smiled and ruffled the boy's hair. "For you, Christopher. You've been a good boy this year, haven't you?"

Nodding, Chris was speechless.

"Old Santa knows that, and he told me to make sure you had one of these fine rabbit traps."

Bursting into ecstatic disbelief, Chris jumped up and down, joy coming out of every pore. Dog barked, joining the celebration.

Ben caught Snood's eye and silently expressed his thanks. No amount of money in the world could buy the joy on his son's face at that moment.

Years later, when Chris built his own son a rabbit trap, he would look back fondly on the Christmas Eve when he learned the true meaning of Christmas in Homer Blott's garage. But for tonight, Ben took joy in this simple act of kindness.

Inside the Blotts' fragrant kitchen, Jody and Peg
sipped cups of warm cider, eyes fixed on the two
women chatting as they worked.

Henrietta and Maxine stood over a huge bowl containing dry bread crumbs, cornmeal mush, chopped
onions, celery, eggs, and sage. Adding salt, pepper,
and hot turkey broth, Maxine buried her hands in the
mixture and tasted, mixed, and tasted again until the
dressing was pronounced just right.

A row of pumpkin and pecan pies sat cooling on the windowsill. Fat, round, yeasty-smelling rolls had been set to rise in pans on the kitchen table. Two flaky brown mincemeat pies—Homer's favorite, Maxine informed them—sat on top of the deep freezer to add to the festivities. Christmas wouldn't be Christmas at the Blotts', the granny-looking woman explained, without mincemeat pie.

Once the plump tom was stuffed and in the oven—Maxine explained that she always cooked the turkey on low all night—she set a big bowl, overflowing with black walnuts still in the shell, on the table. Rummaging through a utensil drawer, she located a couple of small ball peen hammers and two funny-looking long steel picks. When she set the odd tool assortment in front of Jody, the little girl looked lost.

"Nuts for the fudge," Maxine said. "Get to picking, young lady."

For the next half hour, Jody hammered hard shells open and picked pieces of fleshy meat out of hulls. The little girl's face beamed with pleasure; one nut for the bowl, one nut for her mouth set the pace.

Peg looked on, established in Maxine's grand-

daughter's high chair, eating graham crackers. Brownish goo ringed the baby's mouth, and she banged a plastic spoon on the tray, making an awful racket.

Maxine set a pan containing sugar, salt, a pinch of cream of tartar, Karo syrup, Milnot, and cocoa on the stove and turned on the gas jet. When the ingredients reached a rolling boil, she began a strange ritual: dipping a tiny drop of sugary mixture into a cup of cold water, swirling it around, then shaking her head.

"Hasn't formed a soft ball yet."

She hiked the flame a little higher. The rich, thick chocolate smell drenched the kitchen.

Jody cracked and picked, Peg smeared and mashed, Maxine stirred and dropped and Henrietta wielded a warm washcloth, trying in vain to keep up with sticky fingers.

When the magic ball formed, Maxine whisked the pan off the fire, added vanilla flavoring and a dollop of butter, and set the mixture to cool before adding nuts. Motioning for Jody and Henrietta and Peg to follow her, she opened a door off the kitchen and switched on an overhead light. The entourage trooped up the stairs

to the attic with Henrietta carrying Peg and Jody's short legs struggling to keep up.

Wind whistled around the eaves and rattled the outside shutters. The dim attic was cool until Henrietta switched on a small electric heater and warmth spread through the storage area.

Jody's saucer-sized eyes roamed the shadowy interior as she edged closer to Henrietta and latched onto her hand.

The cluttered room contained assorted trunks, discarded lampshades, abandoned chairs, and various odds and ends. A cheval mirror and a sewing form sat in the middle of the room. A huge cutting table covered with gaily wrapped Christmas presents stood in the center of the floor.

"Have to keep presents hidden up here or the grandkids will find them," Maxine explained. "Now," she turned and smiled at Jody. "I don't know of any little girl who can't occupy herself looking through old trunks, do you, Henrietta?"

Henrietta cackled. "Lands no, I used to love to dress up in my mother's clothes—oh, she had such pretty things."

The two women swapped winks.

"Say, Maxine, I bet if we were to open that big ol' trunk over there we'd find all kinds of clothes. What do you say? Want to take a look?"

"Why, Henrietta, that sounds like a fine idea. Say, Jody, maybe you can open the trunk for us?"

Jody's eyes widened, and she broke into a grin. "You want me to open the trunk?"

Grinning, Maxine nodded. "Think there might be some pretties in there."

Henrietta released Peg, who crawled over to join her sister. The young girls struggled to lift the heavy lid, their faces animated with breathless expectancy.

Clothing spilled out of the opened trunk: long earth-colored dresses, colorful feathered hats, heavy coats—even a delicate, time-faded wedding dress.

Squealing, Jody reached for a veil folded in tissue and slipped the lacy article on her head, then jammed her feet into a pair of white satin high heels. She clopped over to stand before the mirror, transfixed by her image.

"Oh, look," she breathed. "I look just like a bride."

Peg wanted in on the fun, so Henrietta located a

small child's skirt and blouse and dressed her. Adding a jaunty hat and umbrella, Henrietta admired her work.

The little girl giggled and crawled and rolled around the attic floor, having no idea what she was doing but having a whale of a time doing it.

Henrietta and Maxine caught the holiday spirit that filled the old attic. After much searching, Maxine came up with a dress popular during the Depression and put it on.

Henrietta sat back on her haunches and roared when Maxine did the lindy, then performed a comical imitation of the Charleston. Getting to her feet, Henrietta joined hands with Maxine in a spirited jitterbug.

Jody whooped and preened and thumped around in high heels and a hat with ostrich feathers while the two older women danced, recalling days of youth.

Breathless, Maxine dropped to her knees in front of the trunk and examined a fur coat that'd seen better days. "Can you believe we really wore this stuff?"

Reaching for the wedding veil Jody had found earlier, Henrietta plopped it on top of her head and sashayed around the room, her horsey laugh drowning out the whistling wind. She paused long enough to drape

a long string of pearls around Jody's neck, then tugged the child and Maxine along behind in train fashion, all three females singing a slightly off-key version of "The Wedding March."

Exhausted from all the excitement, Maxine went back downstairs to the kitchen to finish the fudge. Henrietta and the girls sorted through old photo albums, viewing the Blotts' family history.

"Who's that?" Jody pointed to a stern-looking man with his hat resting across his chest. A rigid, unsmiling woman sat beside him.

"I think that's Maxine's mother and father, hon."

"They look mad."

Laughing, Henrietta pulled the two girls onto her lap and hugged them. "Poor little tykes. You must miss your mommy something awful."

Jody nodded. "I miss Mommy, but I feel sorry for my daddy."

"You do?" The old woman's eyes softened. "Well, honey, it's natural for your daddy to be sad for a while. We know Mommy is with God, but it does make us sad when we lose someone, because we can't be with that person anymore."

"I know—Mommy said Daddy would be sad. But as sad as he feels about Mommy, me and Chris and Peg are making him sadder."

"Sadder?" Henrietta adjusted the child on her lap more comfortably. "Now why would you say that?"

"Daddy's sad because it's Christmas, and he don't have any money to buy us presents—least not many presents. I saw three packages in the car trunk so I know he has presents, just not a lot."

"And that bothers you, little one?"

The little girl turned poignant eyes on Henrietta. "I don't care about presents—Santa will bring me gifts. And he'll bring Chris a train, too, so Daddy shouldn't be sad. Should he? Can you ask my daddy not to be sad, Miss Henrietta?"

Patting the child's head, Henrietta promised softly, "I'll talk to him, darlin'."

And in her wise-beyond-years reasoning, Jody said, "'Cause presents don't make you happy—loving one another makes you happiest of all."

The women returned to the garage, and the men immediately informed them of the traps. Amid a lot of oohing

100

and aahing, everyone agreed they were the finest-looking gifts they'd ever seen.

Chris preened, showing off the rectangular box, the door with the hook, and the shiny nails.

Homer and Lonnie stopped working long enough to enjoy a cup of eggnog Henrietta poured from a large thermos.

As the clock edged toward midnight, Homer and Lonnie finished with the pickup and moved it outside. A few minutes later, the old Mercury was up on jacks, and Ben joined the other two men to pull the transmission.

"We'll get on 'er first thing Tuesday morning," Homer promised as they closed the double doors and the families headed off for home.

Henrietta started the VW. The kids were in the backseat, asleep now. Dog lay on the floorboard, snoring. The eggnog and excitement had worn them all to a frazzle.

"Is there a motel close by?" Ben asked as the bug swerved onto the highway (late night didn't improve Henrietta's driving).

"Nothing around for forty miles. Why?"

"I can't keep imposing on you—me and the kids can rent a hotel—"

"Rent a hotel room? On Christmas Eve?" By the look on Henrietta's face, he realized that he'd insulted her.

She mashed harder on the gas pedal, and the old car chugged along, the heater pumping out warm air. "You'll do no such thing. Why, I'm sure to have at least two or three couples wanting to use the parlor for Christmas vows, and I'll need my witnesses."

"But—"

"No *buts,* young man. Christmas vows are five dollars extra," she reminded. As if that settled the matter, the old woman focused on the road for the remainder of the drive home.

Ben mentally heaved a sigh of relief. He wouldn't have to move the children into an impersonal hotel room and try to keep them occupied until the car was fixed. And he had to admit that spending Christmas at the Marrying Parlor wouldn't be so bad; the old house was warm and comfortable.

Christmas vows five dollars extra.

He cast a sidelong glance at Henrietta. Now why in the *world* would holiday vows cost more?

The holiday spirit settled around the Marrying
Parlor like a comfortable shoe.

All three kids needed a bath after a night in Homer
Blott's garage. Ben thought morning would be soon
enough, but Henrietta said they were too dirty to sleep
well. She supplied a bottle of Joy dishwashing deter-
gent and suggested Ben treat the little ones to a bubble
bath.

Though it was hours past Peg's bedtime, the little girl splashed in the sudsy water, her eyes a vivid turquoise against the backdrop of white bubbles. He wondered if Sheila had ever thought to include bubbles in the baby's nightly ritual. Ben leaned back on his heels, laughing, as the child batted the water, her gummy grin a beacon in the chipped porcelain.

Later, Ben tucked all three children between clean-smelling linens, their cheeks still rosy from hot water and the long day's excitement.

"Tonight's Christmas Eve," Jody reminded, giving an anticipatory shiver. "Do you hear any jingle bells?"

"Not yet," Ben said.

Peg clapped her pudgy hands as though she understood every word.

Christmas Eve. A time when moms and dads tucked reluctant children into bed before starting their night's work. Hours of ratcheting bicycle parts, assembling toys, and the last-minute dash to Wal-Mart for triple- and double-A batteries. There'd be no such scramble for Ben tonight. Earlier, he'd taken the crudely wrapped packages from the Mercury's trunk. It wouldn't take long to get them and lay them beside the bed.

Chris yawned widely, scrunching deeper into the down coverlet. "Are you sure Santa can find us?"

"I'm sure, son—"

"'Cause I sure want my train. It's gonna have a whistle on it, and lots and lots of track, and all these houses and—"

Ben cut him off. "Who says prayer first?"

Ben listened to the simple petitions: God bless Daddy, thank you for the warm bed and the nice woman who lets us stay in her house. Please tell Mommy we miss her really bad.

Jody seemed reluctant to move on. "And God, can you tell Mommy we had fun today? Daddy took us for a walk in Miss Henrietta's pasture and we made snow angels, picked up acorns and leaves, and watched a mommy deer and her baby drinking water from an icy stream. Oh, and God? Tell Mommy we been watching lots of people getting married, and then Daddy puts our name next to his on this funny-looking piece of paper. It's been fun. Daddy says not to worry—Santa Claus will find us tonight, so I'm not worrying. 'Night, Mommy."

Jody yanked the sheet over her head. Chris boiled

from underneath, shaking off the heavy coverlet. A wrestling match ensued, and it took Ben several minutes to get the rowdy pair under control.

Later, Ben tiptoed downstairs to get the presents he'd hidden in the hall closet. He had no present for Henrietta so he'd decided to give her ten dollars of the three hundred and sixty-nine he now had. Ten dollars wouldn't buy much, but he wanted her to have something from him and the kids.

Pans rattled in the kitchen, and he assumed Henrietta was still up.

Creeping into the living room, he sat down in the overstuffed chair in front of the window and watched cotton-ball-sized snowflakes fall from the heavens. White flakes stuck to bare branches and coated tops of fence railings. The sheer beauty of the moment caught Ben's breath. How anyone could say there wasn't a God puzzled him. Irregular-sized flecks danced and skipped across the frozen landscape that only months before must have been lush and green, with brilliant yellow forsythia and budding jonquils. It had taken a master's hand to create such an awesome cycle—spring, summer, fall, and winter. Leaves of burnished gold lay in a shoe box

beside the bed, waiting to be given as a gift to a grand-mother who would press the leaves in an album; the reminder of a granddaughter's love would remain with her long after the season passed.

Henrietta came into the room, her pink slippers slapping against the hardwood floors. Ben smiled, taking the cup of eggnog she offered. "My grandmother's recipe—I'm from German stock, you know."

Ben didn't know. "Thank you. Isn't it late for you to be up?"

"It's Christmas Eve, young man—no one goes to bed early on Christmas Eve."

The old woman eased her sizable bulk into another overstuffed chair, heaving a contented sigh. Wood popped in the blazing fireplace. Tonight, for this moment, Ben's world was at peace.

Companionable silence stretched into the late-night complacency as they sipped thick, creamy eggnog heavily laced with nutmeg.

Henrietta's eyes centered on nature's splendid display taking place outside the window. "You're worried about your kids' Christmas, aren't you?"

Nodding, Ben stared at the falling snow. "My

children have been through a difficult time, Mrs. Humblesmith. I'd hoped that spending Christmas with Mom would help. Now we're not able to do that, though I am deeply grateful for your hospitality."

Henrietta nodded sympathetically, orange juice curlers flopping with the effort.

"Children don't understand death and hard times," Ben said.

Tipping her cup, Henrietta observed quietly, "Death's hard on kiddies, all right, but I wouldn't worry about their Christmas. The nicest things don't always come wrapped in pretty packages."

Ben knew that better than most, but he'd planned on this Christmas being different. Last year he'd been in prison, and the holidays had been bleak. Sheila had taken the bus and brought the kids to visit, but their time together had been short and had taken place in a room filled with a hundred other inmates trying to catch a few minutes of privacy with loved ones. The encounter had left him with a depression he couldn't shake for weeks. He and Sheila wouldn't have had much this year, either, but they would have been together. Sheila made a lot of the kids' presents: knitted caps and gloves. She let them

bake cookies in the oven. Each child would have had a jar of dough with his or her name on it, tied with a pretty red bow and green ribbon. . . .

Ben closed his eyes as pain cut through him. If the transmission had held together a hundred and eighty miles longer, he'd be at Mom's and the house would smell of home.

The Marrying Parlor smelled faintly of nutmeg, plastic flowers, and Henrietta's strongly scented flip-flops.

"It won't be so bad, son," the old woman said softly, as though his thoughts were an open book. "The kids had a good day, didn't they? I thought Jody was going to bust a stitch laughing so hard tonight. Chris loves that old mangy dog. And he took to Snood real well. Have you ever seen a child more excited than your boy when Snood gave him that rabbit trap?"

Ben hadn't—Chris's face had lit up like a neon sign. Time spent building the trap, and Snood's gift, were things Chris would never forget.

Summoning up a smile, Ben pushed out of the chair. "Yes, ma'am—it is late. I'd better turn in; Peg will be up before dawn."

Nodding, Henrietta remained seated, idly sipping from her cup.

Ben climbed the stairs, heavy footed, Jody's excited observation ringing in his ears: *"It's Christmas Eve, Daddy!"*

"Are you sure Santa will find us? I sure want my train. It's going to have a whistle and houses and lots and lots of track...."

"And my new toy kitchen will have a oven with a light...."

Tonight didn't feel like Christmas Eve to Ben; it felt more like the day the warden called him in his office and informed him of Sheila's death.

On Christmas morning Ben slowly opened his eyes, blinking against the harsh glare streaming in from the open curtains. It took a minute for him to orient his thoughts.

Bright sunshine.

The Marrying Parlor.

The children.

Christmas morning.

His hand groped the sheets beside him, and he discovered they were cold. Bolting upright, he stared at the empty side of the bed. Chris, Jody, and Peg were all missing.

Throwing the coverlet aside, he bounded out of bed, grabbing his jeans off the foot of the bed. Hopping across the floor, he shimmied into the denim and flung open the bedroom door.

Had the kids slipped out early, hoping to find a plethora of Christmas presents awaiting them under a nonexistent tree? Chris would be searching for his train; Jody, the Fisher-Price toy kitchen she expected. . . .

Taking the stairs two at a time, Ben fastened his jeans and then pulled on a T-shirt. Excited children's voices came from the living room. The mouthwatering scent of turkey baking in the oven inundated the old house. Throwing the double doors open, Ben gaped at a sight almost beyond description.

A humongous pine tree, standing floor to ceiling, dominated the living room. Festooned with sparkling, miniature white glass balls, strings of popcorn, and holly berries, the spectacle took Ben's breath away. Shiny

silver tinsel hung everywhere. Hundreds of twinkling lights blazed from the stupendous tree.

His eyes switched from the tree to the people standing around the room, faces wreathed in smiles—strangers less than forty-eight hours ago. Snood Grison and a plumpish, pleasant-looking woman with a round face standing beside him. Ed Wingate and his family grouped by the fireplace, welcoming Ben with holiday grins. Homer and Maxine Blott, along with their boy, Lonnie, and his family.

Henrietta stood in the middle of the chaos, clasping little Peg to her ample hip while Chris and Jody scrambled under the tree loaded with gaily wrapped packages.

A toy train, steam rolling from its stack, chugged round and round the Christmas tree, blowing a whistle—a very loud whistle, Ben noted.

When Henrietta spotted him standing in the doorway, the crowd broke into a spirited version of "Deck the Halls."

Once calm reigned again, Henrietta's old features beamed. "We thought you'd grown to the bed!"

Her deep, infectious laugh rang out on the clear,

Christmas morning, rattling the windows of the Marrying Parlor.

Dog sat in the middle of the chaos, watching the festivities with a doggy grin.

Jody rushed over to grab her daddy's hand, her vibrant face flushed with excitement. "Look, Daddy! Santa *did* find us!"

Ben's eyes followed the little girl, who was now propelling him toward a toy kitchen display Martha Stewart would envy. His mouth worked, but he was unable to form words. Emotion twisted into a tight knot in his throat. What had Henrietta done? She must have been up all night putting up the tree, wrapping presents, stuffing turkey. What had the people of this small, caring community sacrificed in order to be here this morning, sharing their Christmas with a stranded family?

Henrietta recognized his emotional state and calmly took his arm and pulled him into the room.

Kids roamed about, shiny eyes aglow with Christmas morning awe.

"Everyone find a seat!" Henrietta called. "It's Santa time!"

A terrible racket erupted in a flurry of jingle bells.

114

A red-suited Santa with a flowing white beard and a belly that shook like a bowl full of jelly bounded down the stairway. *"Ho, ho, ho! Merry Christmas!"*

Older children jumped up and down, while younger, wide-eyed kids ran for the closest parent. Presents flowed, packages dressed in red, gold, and silver. Packages covered with Santa Claus paper or paper with holly and wreaths or toy soldiers were bandied about.

Ben protested as gifts started to pile up by his chair: gloves, a flashlight from the Blotts, a set of screwdrivers from Snood Grison, and a small Bible from the Wingates.

The kids tore into packages of crayons, coloring books, Play-Doh, and board games—so many that Ben lost count. Maxine Blott had wrapped a pair of women's white satin high-heeled shoes and given them to Jody. The little girl squealed with delight when she unwrapped the peculiar gift.

Each child received a brand-new pair of much-needed snow boots. And a hat and warm mittens. Dog even got a rubber bone and a box of Liv-A Snaps. The children had so many presents Ben almost forgot to get the ones he'd purchased, from upstairs, beside the bed.

The train went round and round the tree, *toooooot, tooooooot*ing. Chris jumped up and down, his eyes following the train's path, pure joy dancing in his eyes.

"How?" Ben finally managed when Henrietta dropped down into the chair beside him, bouncing Peg on her knee.

"The train? Shucks, that was my boy, Paul's. Santa brought it to him when he was around six—just been waiting for a chance to drag it out again. And the toy kitchen belonged to one of Lonnie Blott's young'uns. There are a few pieces missing, and Katie ate the handle on the stove and had to be rushed to the emergency room last year, but I doubt Jody will ever notice."

"Henrietta, I appreciate the train and kitchen more than you'll ever know, but Chris and Jody will want to take the toys home. . . ."

The children were so happy with the long-anticipated gifts that Ben wouldn't have the heart to take them away. He'd have to pay Henrietta and the Blotts—

"Why, sure they will! The gifts are theirs to keep!"

"But the train belongs to your son," Ben gently pointed out. "He will want it for his son—your grandson."

"Well . . . he might," she conceded. The old woman leaned closer, an angelic light filling her eyes. "But to be honest, he never cared much for the train. Liked a fire engine his grandma Bills gave him a lot more. Don't be afraid to accept help, Ben. Gifts given in love deserve cordial acceptance," she reminded. "Don't you know? Joy is in the giving *and* receiving. I used to think that *things* could buy happiness, but this past year I've come to know that love is the only real happiness. It's the best kind of joy, and when you can give it, it's better than getting—any day of the week."

She settled back in her chair, staring at the winter wonderland outside the living-room window. "Sometimes a body goes to extra lengths to provide happiness, but in my opinion, the effort is worth every ounce the bother."

Ben's heart felt as if it were going to burst with affection for this woman and the values she had taught him during his brief stay at the Marrying Parlor. Henrietta loved people, and she dedicated her life to spreading joy. Not many could make the same claim.

Shortly after the last gift was opened, Homer, Lonnie, and Snood excused themselves, saying they had

an errand to run. Noon rolled around, and the men still weren't back. By one o'clock the kids were getting hungry, so the women decided to eat without the men.

"Homer's used to warming his meal in the microwave," Maxine said with a fatalistic shrug.

The turkey was sliced, dressing and gravy dished up and poured. Potatoes were mashed, and sweet potatoes heaped and topped with browned marshmallows. Salads—both gelatin and green—golden corn, green beans, hot tamale pie, crusty brown yeast rolls, and rich creamy butter filled the groaning table. Afterward, pumpkin, pecan, and mincemeat pie made the rounds, over cups of steaming, freshly brewed coffee.

After dinner, the house settled into a lazy holiday atmosphere. Someone switched on the television, and an NFL football game blared. The children sprawled all over the living-room floor in an overfed stupor and played with new toys. Adults read the newspaper. Lonnie Blott's wife, Sue, disappeared into the parlor with Maxine, and a few minutes later Christmas carols erupted from the old pump organ.

"Merry Christmas, Mom." Ben grinned into the phone receiver, balancing Peg on his hip. He moved the mouthpiece closer to Peg, and she produced a ten-month-old *blaaaaaaahhh*—Peg's version of "Merry Christmas, Nana!"

"We've had a great Christmas," Ben assured Thelma. "Homer says he'll have the car running by tomorrow afternoon. We'll have our Christmas when the kids and I get there. . . . I'll drive careful. . . . Sure, I'll put coats on the kids. . . . And hats. Even boots—they all have a pair now."

He grinned. "I love you, too, Mom."

By midafternoon, Ben relaxed in the old chair in front of the window while Peg napped on a pallet beside him. Random flakes drifted from the lead-colored sky. The Christmas tree twinkled merrily in the muted afternoon light. *Oh, Sheila, honey, I wish you could have been here to see this. The kids—*

"Did you and the little ones have a good Christmas?" Henrietta roused him from his musings.

"The best, Mrs. Humblesmith, thank you." He sat up, rubbing his eyes. Ben suddenly realized it *was* a good Christmas—one of the best ever. Henrietta and the whole community had given his family a Christmas they

would never forget; yet oddly enough, the greatest joys had come from the mouth of a child.

Sheila's gift to him, spoken through the innocence of their six-year-old: *"Mommy said when I grow up and get married, I should look for a man exactly like you, because Mommy says you're good to the bone, Daddy."*

The young girl at McDonald's, her gift given with a wink and a meaningful smile: *"Enjoy the fries, sir. Merry Christmas."*

Images floated through his mind like colorful murals.

"Look, Daddy! I think he wants to go home with us." And so they had acquired Dog.

"Me and the boy will get right on that transmission, Ben. We need to get you home for the holidays...."

"Look, Daddy, I'm making an angel!"

"'And while they were there, the time came for her baby to be born. She gave birth to her first child, a son. She wrapped him snugly in strips of cloth and laid him in a manger, because there was no room for them in the village inn.'"

"A rabbit trap, Daddy! Mr. Grison gave me my own rabbit trap!"

"And I cracked nuts and Mrs. Blott put them in the fudge—and then Daddy, I dressed up in a wedding gown and we made this funny train, singing a wedding song...."

"My train! Santa did find me!"

"See Daddy, the oven has a light, just like I wanted. Isn't Santa nice!"

"Blaaaaaaahhh. Merry Christmas, Nana!"

Tears welled in Ben's eyes. Christmas wasn't about bicycles and dolls and new appliances. He had spent the last couple of days worrying that the children's Christmas would be less because he couldn't afford to give more.

Instead, God, in the form of the Blotts, Snood Grison, the Wingates, and Henrietta Humblesmith, had given him gifts in the ordinary experiences that would remain in his heart long after the tree had come down and the brightly colored tinsel and wrapping paper had been carefully stored away until next season.

The birth of a Savior and hope for the future.

Friends, strangers. Odd-looking wedding parlors and glimpses of a child's heart. That's what Christmas was about.

Henrietta's front door opened, and the missing men

122

stomped in, shaking snow off their boots. Now dressed in grease-stained coveralls, they shouted, "Where's the beef?"

Or turkey, on this particular occasion.

Maxine and Sue poured out of the Marrying Parlor. Henrietta jumped to her feet and started grabbing dishes of food out of the refrigerator and sticking them into the microwave while Lucille Wingate gathered clean plates.

Snood and Homer headed for the living room, shouting Ben's name. Ben got up and came to stand in the living-room doorway.

Snood sobered. "Come out here, son. We got something we want to show you."

Lonnie took hold of Ben's arm, and the men moved him to the front porch. Women and children followed, wrapping their hands around forearms to ward off the chill.

The old Mercury was idling in the driveway, smoke rolling from the rusted tailpipe.

Ben blinked. "My car?"

Snood and Homer broke into grins, their eyes lit with mischief. Homer cleared his throat. "We figured if all three of us got on it, we could have those bands and pump back in the transmission by midafternoon." The mechanic slapped Ben on the back good-naturedly. "The way we figure it, you can be home by seven or a little after. Won't be like spending the whole day with your mom, but you'll have a few hours of Christmas left." Glancing at Lonnie, he winked. "And you can have your Christmas dinner."

Ben slumped against the snow-covered porch banister, overcome with gratitude. Had he said he'd had a good Christmas?

A knot the size of a wishbone crowded Ben O'Keefe's throat. It was the best Christmas.

The O'Keefes celebrated Christmas twice that year: once at the Marrying Parlor and later with Mom.

They arrived in Poplar Bluff (with Dog) around nine o'clock Christmas evening. The look on Mom's face was present enough for Ben. She made coffee in her Mr. Coffee, and they ate thick pieces of pumpkin pie with whipped cream on top, both Ben and Thelma marveling at how Chris and Jody had grown since the last time she had seen them. She got acquainted with Peg, and it was after one before the lights went out and the tired family settled down on a cold winter's night.

Ben stepped over dirty patches of snow as he walked to work two months later. God had been good. He'd found a job at a local garage the week after Christmas. The hours were good, and the pay was fair. He'd rented a two-room efficiency two blocks from Mom's, where he and the kids now lived. Jody was in school, and he'd found a retired schoolteacher to look after Chris and Peg during the day.

A raw March wind buffeted the young man as he ducked into the diner for breakfast. Six o'clock in the morning found only a few customers occupying faded plastic booths.

"The usual, Ben?" Madge Garrett called. She filled a yawning patron's coffee cup.

"You got it, Madge." Ben slid onto the stool, reaching for a copy of the *Daily American Republic*.

Stepping behind the lunch counter, Madge picked

up another cup and set it in front of him. Pouring the strong brew, she smiled. "How's the job going?"

Smiling, Ben added cream to the steaming cup. "Real good. I guess I'm a fair shade-tree mechanic."

"Rumor is you're better than fair, mister." The blonde winked. "Stop selling yourself short."

Ben grinned, his eyes returning to the morning news. The usual dominated the headlines: war, rumors of war, prosperity, hints of recession. Flipping to the sports section, he noted that the Lady Mules had won their tournament. Way to go, Lady Mules.

Breakfast arrived—two eggs over medium, sausage, hash browns, biscuits and gravy. He absently reached for the salt when his eye caught a tiny article on page five. The caption read: Distraught Daughter Defends Daring Mother.

Spooning eggs into his mouth, Ben read on, his eyes widening in disbelief.

Beth Hargus, daughter of Henrietta Humble-smith, proprietor of the Marrying Parlor located twenty miles outside of Memphis, attempted to explain her mother's bizarre

actions today at a local news conference. The daughter claims that Mrs. Humblesmith intended no harm when she neglected to acquire a license to perform nuptials. "Mother loves people and wants to see them happy," Mrs. Hargus was quoted as saying. "Loneliness, especially around the holidays, can drive people to do strange things," the daughter lamented. "My brother and I should have been more aware of Mother's activities and temporary lack of judgment."

Charges for Henrietta Humblesmith are pending, but prosecutors speculate that Mrs. Humblesmith will face a hefty fine in lieu of jail time. Be advised that couples married between the months of November 1999 and February 2000 should take immediate action. Vows taken at the Marrying Parlor were not legal, and appropriate measures should be taken to correct the mistake.

Or not.

Vows taken any time in the week leading up to Christmas at the Marrying Parlor included

an additional five-dollar fee, which, Henrietta's daughter said, "went to the church offering on Christmas Eve."

Ben whistled softly, an ornery grin spreading across his handsome features. Henrietta? Marrying folks without a license? He thought of the kind old woman who wanted nothing more than to witness love on people's faces. And he supposed worse things could happen. "You may have cut a few corners, Henrietta, but in my book, you're an angel."

Sobering, Ben O'Keefe wondered exactly how many angels God had sent him this Christmas.

A few, Ben conceded, closing his eyes briefly to thank the Lord. *More than a few.*

RECIPES

Henrietta's Holiday Eggnog

⅓ cup sugar
3 egg yolks
Pinch of salt
4 cups half-and-half
    (it's Christmas—fat grams don't count)
2 egg whites
3 tablespoons sugar
1 teaspoon vanilla or rum flavoring to taste
1 cup whipping cream, whipped
Ground nutmeg to taste

Combine sugar, egg yolks, and salt in a large bowl; stir in half-and-half. Stir constantly until mixture coats the spoon; set aside. Beat egg whites until foamy. Gradually add three tablespoons sugar, beating to form soft peaks. Combine with the custard mixture; add vanilla or rum flavoring. Chill six hours. Serve with whipped cream and nutmeg.

Maxine Blott's Cocoa Fudge

3 cups sugar
3/4 cup Milnot evaporated milk
3 tablespoons cocoa
4 tablespoons Karo syrup
1/8 teaspoon cream of tartar
Dash of salt
1 teaspoon vanilla
Dollop of butter

Combine all the ingredients except butter and vanilla in a saucepan and cook to a rolling boil. Boil and stir until mixture forms a soft ball when dropped into a cup of cold water. Remove from heat, add vanilla and butter, and let cool for about 15 minutes; then beat until creamy. Add nuts (black walnuts are the best), if desired, and pour into buttered pan. Cut when cool.

ABOUT THE AUTHOR

Lori Copeland has published more than fifty novels and has won numerous awards for her books. Publishing with Tyndale House allows her the freedom to write stories that express her love of God and her personal convictions.

Lori lives with her wonderful husband, Lance, in Springfield, Missouri. She has three incredibly handsome grown sons, three absolutely gorgeous daughters-in-law, and five exceptionally bright grandchildren—but then, she freely admits to being partial when it comes to her family. Lori enjoys reading biographies, attending book discussion groups, and participating in morning water-aerobic exercises at the local YMCA, and she is presently trying very hard to learn to play bridge. She loves to travel and is always thrilled to meet her readers.

When asked what one thing Lori would like others to know about her, she readily says, "I'm not perfect—just forgiven by the grace of God." Christianity to Lori means peace, joy, and the knowledge that she has a

Friend, a Savior, who never leaves her side. Through her books, she hopes to share this wondrous assurance with others.

BOOKS BY LORI COPELAND